The Purple Turtle

Modi's Magical Adventures

Written by Tamera Fair & Tonia Evans

To order additional copies of this book, contact:
Xlibris
844-714-8691
www.Xlibris.com
Orders@Xlibris.com

Library of Congress Control Number: 2023910456
ISBN: Softcover   978-1-6698-7981-7
        Hardcover   978-1-6698-7977-0
        EBook   978-1-6698-7982-4

Print information available on the last page

Rev. date: 08/07/2023

Modi loved being outdoors. She smelled every flower she passed.
She named the birds and the squirrels; she even loved the grass.

She tended to the rose bushes, and the trees who kept her busy.
She walked and talked in the backyard, with nature, until she was happily dizzy.

Their beauty made her smile with their aroma and beautiful sights.
Even when it was gloomy outside, their colors shined bright.

When winter came the snow grew deeper until it blanketed her garden.
It covered the sleeping flowers as they awaited the spring to unthaw them.

When the snow finally reached her bedroom window, Modi grew very lonely.
Without her friends to see every day, the cold was her one and only.

A pet would be a great companion, one day she did decide.
Her mom and dad took her to the shelter when it was safe to drive outside.

Modi saw so many fluffy puppies she could one day adore!
Including a white cocker spaniel that woofed and licked the floor.

A speckled shih tzu with large eyes drooping at the door,
And a sleeping yellow lab, boy did he snore!

There was a feisty silky terrier, who just yapped and yapped.
But most of them just lay around looking tired and tapped.

"Maybe a cat?" she asked her folks who guided her to the opposite side.
People treated some animals badly. That she could not abide!

She saw an exotic-looking Siamese cat, who strutted the floor with pride.
There was a Persian kitten with fabulous greenish-gray eyes.

Nearby lay an orange tabby cat so handsome, he could win a prize.
How could she choose just one?
For the longest time, she just couldn't decide!

"We can make them all happy because we have a big house and a big yard."
"Sorry sweetie," her mom replied, "one pet only is the shelter's safeguard."

"You don't have to decide today," dad said, "if it is too tough."
It was too much for Modi, so she left feeling stuck.

Without a new pet in her arms, it was a very quiet and sad drive home.
The snow began to fall again from the sky, creating a beautiful white dome.

As the days passed, Modi thought about getting a rabbit, soft and oh-so fluffy.
With his adorable big ears and twitching nose, she could name him Snuffy!

It would be the perfect pet, and she imagined it sleeping in her room.
Walking with him in the yard when spring finally bloomed.

But mom and dad thought the cage would smell, and the rabbit would be destructive.
Eating wooden furniture, and the mess! It wouldn't be very productive.

"I want a pet I can hold and love, which sleeps in my room," Modi cried.
She felt sad again and loneliness crept back in her heart to hide.

Spring came with thunder and rain, which turned the garden into a muddy mess.
Modi's smile disappeared, and she walked to and from school in total sadness.

Since the weather was not cooperative, Modi missed playing with her garden friends.
She sulked about the rabbit she would never get, and the rain that never ends.

Then daddy came to her room to say, "Honey, I know you're sad, but please don't worry.
When the right pet comes along you'll know it. It may not even be furry!"

"Having patience is hard sometimes, but it will be worth the wait.
You will find that one true friend, and it will be oh so great."

He continued. "Look at the flowers outside, they wait for the sun to show.
They stay waiting patiently for warm rays that will help them grow."

Eventually, they'll bloom. And it's the same for your dreams and what you hope for.
One day soon, you'll see patience is a good thing and will have to wait no more.

On Modi's birthday, mommy came home with a white box wrapped in a beautiful purple bow. A gift! Modi smiled for the first time in a long time. Her mood instantly began to shift.

When she pulled apart the ribbon and lifted the lid, she saw him...a purple turtle! An animal unlike any she had ever seen. He reminded her of mom's friend, Myrtle.

She ran to her room and put his tank on the bed, gently lifting the turtle into her hand. His sparkling eyes met Modi's as he gave her a big smile. It felt like she was in dreamland.

Daddy was right. You were worth waiting for. You're the perfect pet for me. "Thank you, momma, for the best surprise I'm going to name him Grapie!"

Momma smiled and hugged her close, her smile filled with glee. "His color reminded me of your eyes, it was surely meant to be!"

16

Modi loved Grapie! Every moment she spent with him made her happy.
She always kept him close, right next to her bed. He made her feel squishy and sappy!

Each morning she greeted him, "Good morning, Grapie," and each night with, "I love you."
He always smiled at her when she held him, and she knew he loved her too.

Modi was so happy she started to play with her friends again.
And with the shelter's help, started a pet-adoption campaign.

Every pet needed love, and there were lots to go around.
The world is brighter with a pet, and she knew what she had found.

Modi introduced Grapie to her outdoor friends, and let him swim in the water fountain.
The birds came to say hello as he climbed a small rock that, for him, was like a mountain.

For show and tell one day, Modi's teacher allowed Grapie to come to school.
The other kids loved the turtle a lot. They thought he was super cool.

They invited Grapie back again and again because he was just so super.
He loved all the kids and took the attention like a trooper.

But Grapie belonged to Modi, and he was special to her alone,
He trusted her and she trusted him. They loved their time on their own.

And then something magical happened one night when
Modi whispered "Goodnight Grapie, I love you."

The purple turtle replied in a clear, beautiful voice,
"Goodnight sweet Modi, I love you too!"

WHAT? A TALKING TURTLE!

22

THE AUTHORS

Tamera Fair

Tamera is a Chicago native who has always had an affection for children of all ages. She began her career at the age of twelve while babysitting for a family member with young children. After careful deliberation about her career choices, she weighed her options of becoming a pediatrician or lawyer against becoming an educator. Education won! She launched her first early childcare facility in her early twenties. One facility turned into many. She currently owns and operates a chain of child-care centers in Chicago, is a cohost to the popular daily radio show on iHeart Radio (The Brunch Bunch) on Inspiration 1390, an actress, producer, activist, author and mother.

The Purple Turtle ˜ Adventures of Modi is a six part book series, which chronicles the whimsical adventures of a little girl who receives a rare purple turtle. Modi discovers her turtle can talk and Grapie introduces her to a magical life filled with unicorns, mermaids, and other mystical creatures that make Modi's life adventures even more unique.

Tonia Evans

Tonia Evans was born in Mississippi but raised in the Englewood area on the South Side of Chicago. She is a successful product of the Chicago Public School system and attended Southern University in Carbondale, Illinois. She has always exhibited a devotion to childhood learning, which led her to become a successful director at the Premier Childcare Centers, located throughout the Chicagoland area. Her hard work and dedication as an Early Childhood Education Director has not only allowed Tonia to build a team of successful professionals but has allowed her to nurture this fondness for learning in her first love and son, Joshua.

Print rich environments have always been a must-have in every center I have taught or directed. That has been my motivation to co-write *The Purple Turtle* and bring the classroom alive through Grapie's magical adventures.

Printed in the United States
by Baker & Taylor Publisher Services